113

Harry and the Horse

by Sue Graves

Illustrated by Michael Garton

W
FRANKLIN WATTS

Notes on the series

TIDDLERS are structured to provide support for children who are starting to read on their own. The stories may also be used for sharing with children.

Starting to read alone can be daunting. **TIDDLERS** help by listing the words in the book for a check before reading, and by providing visual support and repeating words and phrases. These books will both develop confidence and encourage reading and rereading for pleasure.

If you are reading this book with a child, here are a few suggestions:

1. Make reading fun! Choose a time to read when you and the child are relaxed and have time to share the story.
2. Talk about the story before you start reading. Look at the cover and the blurb. What might the story be about? Why might the child like it?
3. Look also at the list of words below - can the child tackle most of the words?
4. Encourage the child to retell the story, using the jumbled picture puzzle.
5. Give praise! Remember that small mistakes need not always be corrected.

Here is a list of the words in this story.

Common words:

a	he	this
and	is	to
at	it	up
back	on	was
down	said	went
got	the	

Other words:

Harry	faster	sea
horse	magic	trees
fair	over	under

Harry was at the fair.

He got on
a horse.

5

The horse went
up and down.

It went faster ...

10

... and faster!

13

It went over
the trees.

Magic

It went under
the sea.

It went back
to the fair.

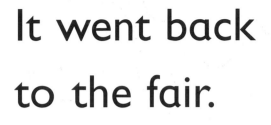

"It was magic!"
said Harry.

Puzzle Time

Can you find these
pictures in the story?

Which pages are the
pictures from?

Turn over for answers!

Answers

The pictures come
from these pages:

a. pages 12 and 13

b. pages 4 and 5

c. pages 16 and 17

d. pages 6 and 7

First published in 2010 by
Franklin Watts
338 Euston Road
London
NW1 3BH

Franklin Watts Australia
Level 17/207 Kent Street
Sydney
NSW 2000

Text © Sue Graves 2010
Illustration © Michael Garton 2010

The rights of Sue Graves to be
identified as the author and Michael Garton
as the illustrator of this Work have been
asserted in accordance with the Copyright,
Designs and Patents Act, 1988.

A CIP catalogue record for this book is
available from the British Library.

ISBN 978 0 7496 9387 9 (hbk)
ISBN 978 0 7496 9399 2 (pbk)

Series Editor: Jackie Hamley
Editor: Melanie Palmer
Series Advisor: Catherine Glavina
Series Designer: Peter Scoulding

Printed in China

Franklin Watts is a division of Hachette Children's Books,
an Hachette UK company. www.hachette.co.uk